THIS BOOK IS DEDICATED TO SCARLETT & HENRY LEE

MUSIC CREDITS:

"We're Going to be Friends"
Performed by The White Stripes | Produced by Jack White
Vocals, Guitar: Jack White | Drums: Meg White
Engineered by Stewart Sikes | Mastered by Fred Kevorkian | Mixed by Jack White, Stewart Sikes
Written by Jack White | Peppermint Stripe Music (BMI), Administered by Songs of Universal, Inc. (BMI)
Recorded at Easley-McCain Recording in Memphis, Tennessee winter 2001 | Mastered at Absolute Audio
The White Stripes and Jack White are managed exclusively worldwide by Monotone, Inc.

"We're Going to be Friends"
Performed by April March | Produced by April March | Arranged by Mehdi Zannad (Fugu)
Vocals: April March | Guitars, Bass, Drums, Shoe, Percussion: Benjamin Glibert (Aquaserge) | Percussion: Mehdi Zannad (Fugu)
Trombone: Rémy Galichet | Ocarina, Soprano Sax: Rémi Sciuto
Engineered and mixed by Frédéric Deces
Recorded in Paris, France at Les Studios du Futur de l'Audiovisuel

"Amis Pour La Vie"
Lyrics translated by Elinor Blake; Mehdi Zannad (Fugu) | Produced by April March | Arranged by Mehdi Zannad (Fugu)
Vocals: April March | Guitars, Bass, Drums, Shoe, Percussion: Benjamin Glibert (Aquaserge) | Percussion: Mehdi Zannad (Fugu)
Trombone: Rémy Galichet | Ocarina, Soprano Sax: Rémi Sciuto
Engineered and mixed by Frédéric Deces
Recorded in Paris, France at Les Studios du Futur de l'Audiovisuel

"We're Going to be Friends"
Performed by Woodstation Elementary School Singers
Directed by Kevin Lane and Jeanna Vaughn
Recorded in the Blue Room, Third Man Records, Nashville, Tennessee

ACKNOWLEDGEMENTS:

jack white would like to thank: meg white, stewart sikes, and meg's silvertone guitar.

Elinor Blake would like to thank: Jack White, Meg White, Chet Weise, Nat Strimpopulos, Kim Baugh, Lucian Zanes, Piero Zanes, Sarah Blake, Whitney Blake, Tony Fucile, George Barkin, Brenda Bowen, Wendi Gu, Mehdi Zannad, Benjamin Glibert, Staci Slater, Stacy Fass, Susan Lee, Lou Doillon, Pierre-François Carron & Jeni Mahoney.

PHOTO PERMISSIONS:

Lou Doillon photo by Denis Rouvre | Sun Etching by Andrea Baccii (15th century Public Domain), Universal History Archive | Sharon, CT Clock Tower photo by David Cunningham | Son House photo by Tom Copi, Michael Ochs Archives | Biblio Burro photo by Nuestro Proyecto Social | American Miniature Donkey Foal photo by Bildagentur Zoonar | Peppermint photos by kristinekreations | Walt Whitman Schoolhouse photos by Samuel H. Gottscho | Clark Park Scoreboard photo by Roe Peterhans | Warstic Baseball Bat photo by Warstic Sports Inc | White Rabbit Herald by Sir John Tenniel (Public Domain) | Betty Boop appears courtesy of Fleischer Studios; photo by Hake's Americana & Collectibles | An Antique Classroom in a Ghost Mining Town photo by Pete Ryan, the National Geographic Collection

TMB017

LIBRARY OF CONGRESS CATALOGING-IN-PUBLICATION DATA

Names: White, Jack, 1975- author. | Blake, Elinor, 1965- illustrator.
Title: We're going to be friends / written by Jack White; illustrations by Elinor Blake.
Other titles: We are going to be friends
Description: First edition. | Nashville, Tennessee: Third Man Books, [2017] | Summary: Based on the song by the lead singer and guitarist of The White Stripes, a girl and boy become friends at the beginning of the school year, and engage in activities in and out of school.
Identifiers: LCCN 2017029062 | ISBN 9780996401692 (hardback)
Subjects: LCSH: Children's songs, English--United States--Texts. | CYAC: Friendship--Songs and music. | Schools--Songs and music. | Songs.
Classification: LCC PZ8.3.W58766 We 2017 | DDC 782.42 [E] --dc23
LC record available at https://lccn.loc.gov/2017029062

For more info: https://thirdmanbooks.com/wgtbf/
Password: booksandpens

FIRST EDITION
ISBN 978-0-9964016-9-2

THIRD MAN BOOKS

WE'RE GOING TO BE FRIENDS

written by JACK WHITE
illustrated by ELINOR BLAKE

fall is here, hear the yell

back

to

school,

ring

the

bell

brand new shoes,

walking blues

climb the fence, books and pens

I can tell that we

are gonna be friends

I can tell that we are gonna be friends

walk with me Suzy Lee

through the park and by the tree

we will rest upon the ground

and look at all the bugs we found

safely walk to school

without a sound

safely walk to school without a sound

here we are, no one else

we walked to school all by ourselves

there's dirt on our uniforms

from chasing all the ants and worms

we clean up and now it's time to learn

we clean up and now it's time to learn

numbers, letters, learn to spell

nouns, and books, and show and tell

playtime we will throw the ball

back to class, through the hall

teacher marks our height against the wall

and we don't notice any time pass

we don't notice anything

we sit side by side in every class

teacher thinks that I sound funny

but she likes the way you sing

tonight I'll dream while I'm in bed

when silly thoughts go through my head

about the bugs and alphabet

and when I wake tomorrow I'll bet

that you and I will walk together again

I can tell that we are gonna be friends

yes, I can tell that we are gonna be friends

THE END